The Magic School Bus®

A Science FACT FINDER

SKELETONS

SCHOLASTIC INC.

New York   Toronto   London   Auckland   Sydney
Mexico City   New Delhi   Hong Kong   Buenos Aires

Written by Jackie Glassman.

Cover illustrations by Linda Nye and Carolyn Bracken.
Interior illustrations by Carisa Swenson, Ted Enik, and Carolyn Bracken.

Based on *The Magic School Bus* books
written by Joanna Cole and illustrated by Bruce Degen.

This book is a nonfiction companion
to *The Magic School Bus: The Search for the Missing Bones.*

The author would like to thank Kammy Fehrenbacher of Columbia
University for her expert advice in reviewing this manuscript.

No part of this publication may be reproduced, or stored in a retrieval system, or transmitted in any form or by any means, electronic, mechanical, photocopying, recording, or otherwise, without written permission of the publisher. For information regarding permission, write to Scholastic Inc., Attention: Permissions Department, 555 Broadway, New York, NY 10012.

ISBN 0-439-31436-4

12 11 10 9 8 7 6 5 4 3 2   2/0 3/0 4/0 5/0 6/0

Cover designed by Carisa Swenson
Interior designed by Madalina Stefan

Printed in the U.S.A.   40

First Scholastic printing, January 2002

Contents

A Note from Ms. Frizzle

Dear Readers,

Before my class boards the Magic School Bus, I always do my research. I find out as much as I can about where we are going and what we will learn there.

When we went on <u>The Search for the Missing Bones</u>, I came ready with everything there is to know about skeletons. My students also deserve a good deal of credit. They discovered a lot about skeletons, too. No bones about it, by the end of the trip, we were all real skeleton experts.

We are excited to share all we have learned from our skeleton unit. You can use the facts you read about here in a report of your own.

Good luck,
Ms. Frizzle

FACT FINDER

SKELETONS

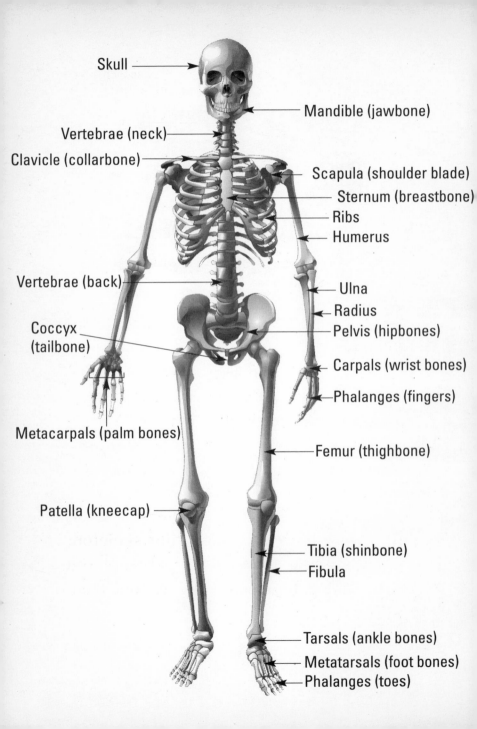

Skull

Mandible (jawbone)

Vertebrae (neck)

Clavicle (collarbone)

Scapula (shoulder blade)

Sternum (breastbone)

Ribs

Humerus

Vertebrae (back)

Ulna

Radius

Pelvis (hipbones)

Coccyx (tailbone)

Carpals (wrist bones)

Phalanges (fingers)

Metacarpals (palm bones)

Femur (thighbone)

Patella (kneecap)

Tibia (shinbone)

Fibula

Tarsals (ankle bones)

Metatarsals (foot bones)

Phalanges (toes)

According to my research, Chapter 1 tells you all the bone basics.

Chapter 1

The Bare Bones

Can you imagine what it would be like if you had no bones inside you? You'd be a heap of muscle and tissue, like a big glob of jelly, all soft and wiggly. Bones give your body its shape. Without your bones, you wouldn't be able to walk, talk, eat, dance, ride your bike, or do anything. You wouldn't be able to move at all.

Luckily you do have bones. Together, all of your bones make up your skeleton. Your skeleton holds your body up, the same way a tent pole keeps a tent from falling down.

Not every living animal has an internal skeleton. Long before human beings existed, there were animals without bones. These boneless creatures, known as invertebrates, include insects, worms, sponges, and jellyfish. The first invertebrates appeared about 700 million years ago. Humans have been on Earth only about 6 million years.

How Many Bones?

There are more than 200 bones that make up your skeleton. Actually, you were born with a lot more than 200 bones. Babies have closer to 350 bones — but don't worry, you didn't lose any. As your body grows bigger, some of the bones join together, so by the time you are an adult you have exactly 206.

When two bones grow into one, scientists say the bones fuse together.

Bones come in all different sizes. Some are huge, like your thighbone. And others are really tiny, like your ear bones.

Bones come in all different shapes, too. Feel one of your arm bones, then one of your ribs. Compare them. You might have noticed that they feel different. That's because arm bones are round, while ribs are flat. Now try comparing other bones. How do your thumb bones feel compared to your shoulder? Does your skull feel different than your knee? The giant thighbone, called the femur, is the largest bone in your body. It makes up one-quarter of a person's height.

The femur is 1/4 as long as a human is tall.

The stirrup, a bone inside your ear, is less than 1/8 inch long.

Keesha's femur is 1 foot (30 cm) long, so she must be about 4 feet (120 cm) tall!

The tiniest bone in your body is an ear bone called the *stirrup*. It is only 0.12 inch (3 mm) long. It vibrates to carry sound into the inner ear so you can hear.

Big or small, round or flat, all bones are hard and strong. But if bones are so hard and strong, why don't they weigh you down and make it hard to move? The answer is that bones are not hard all the way through. Inside the middle part of the bone is a substance called *marrow*. Inside the ends of bones is a lightweight substance called *spongy bone*.

Bones make up less than twenty percent of your body weight.

4

What Are Bones Made Of?

Your bones are made up of three parts:

1) compact bone
2) spongy bone
3) bone marrow

■ Compact Bone:

The hard outside, or exterior, is called *compact bone*. The mineral *calcium* makes compact bone hard and strong. Ninety-nine percent of the calcium in your body is found in your bones.

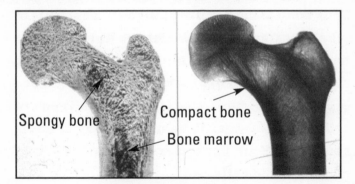

Spongy bone

Compact bone

Bone marrow

Milk, cheese, broccoli, and soybeans are good sources of calcium!

■ Spongy Bone:

There is spongy bone inside the ends of some bones. *Spongy bone* looks like a sponge, but it's not soft or squishy. Its honeycomb design keeps bones strong but light.

■ Bone Marrow:

The red and yellow jellylike stuff inside some bones is called *bone marrow*. Blood cells are made primarily in the red bone marrow.

Your Body's Building Blocks

Your body is made up of billions of tiny cells of all shapes and sizes. Different kinds of cells have different jobs. Muscle cells make up muscles, blood cells make up blood, and bone cells produce bone tissue. All these types of cells work together to keep your body running smoothly. Your bone marrow has the job of making blood cells.

Busy Bones

Next time someone calls you "lazybones," you can explain that bones are far from lazy! In fact, bones are very busy doing lots of important jobs that help to keep your body healthy.

Bones Protect

Some of your bones act like armor to protect your body. Your skull, for example, is like a bike helmet, protecting your brain from getting hurt. Similarly, the spine in your back covers the nerves in your spinal cord. Your ribs are like a cage surrounding your heart, lungs, and

Your bones can protect you, but it's always good to protect your bones when playing sports.

Is this enough protection?

stomach, which helps to keep these soft organs safe.

What Are Organs?

An *organ* is a part of the body that does a particular job. Our organs help us breathe, digest food, excrete, and more. Some organs are:

- Lungs
- Liver
- Intestine
- Heart
- Stomach
- Pancreas
- Liver
- Bladder

Bones Are for Storage

Besides protecting your organs, your bones also act as a storage place for minerals. When other parts of your body need certain minerals, your bones release them into your blood. In addition, yellow bone marrow collects fat and releases it so your body can burn it for energy.

Bones Produce Blood Cells

Red bone marrow makes red and white blood cells. Over two million new blood cells are made every second in the

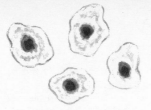

white blood cells

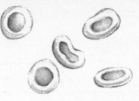

red blood cells

marrow of some of your bones. Red blood cells carry important substances such as oxygen and nutrients to the rest of the body. White blood cells fight infection and disease.

Red blood cells live for only four months, which is why your bones are very busy making new cells all the time.

Platelets, the smallest blood cells, are also produced in the marrow. Platelets help the blood to clot when you are bleeding. Producing blood cells is a very important job for bones.

In order to transport the new blood cells to the rest of the body, bones have blood vessels. Blood vessels allow blood to travel through your bones, transporting important nutrients to and from your bone cells.

Where Blood Cells Are Made

Active red bone marrow that produces blood cells is found primarily in the ends of the long bones, like your upper leg, and in flat bones, like your ribs, skull, and vertebrae.

On top of all these jobs your bones have to do, they also help you grow. To find out more about how bones grow, read on!

Your bones are always on the grow.

Chapter 2
Growing Bones

Bones may look lifeless, but they are very much alive. The living cells inside your bones help you grow. From the age of four to eleven, people grow about 2 to 3 inches (5 to 8 cm) a year. Then, most people have a growth spurt between ages twelve and sixteen when their growth rate increases. But believe it or not, you did most of your growing during your first two years of life.

When babies are born, their bones aren't hard and strong like an adult's. A baby's skeleton is mostly made of a soft, solid, flexible material called *cartilage*. Because cartilage is flexible, babies are less likely to break their bones. However, most of that cartilage will turn to bone as a person grows up. This process is called *ossification,* and it ends around the time that you are fourteen to seventeen years old.

Case of the Missing Cartilage

Most of the cartilage in a baby's body turns to bone, but some cartilage remains even after that baby becomes an adult. The cartilage inside your outer ears and on the tip of your nose, for example, won't ever become bone. That's why you can squish and bend those body parts. Cartilage can also be found where bones come together at joints. This cartilage cushions bones so they don't rub together.

How Do Your Bones Know to Grow?

As you grow taller, your bones are growing longer, especially your leg bones. Chemicals called *growth hormones* are released by your brain. Growth hormones send messages to the cells in your body — including bone cells — telling them when and how much you should grow. Most people grow to between 5 and 6 feet (1.5 m to 1.8 m tall), and reach their maximum height by their early twenties at the latest.

Tallest and Shortest

The tallest person in the world grew to a whopping 8 feet 11 inches (2.7 m).

The shortest person in the world grew to only 22.5 (.6 m) inches.

This composite photo shows two men with growth disorders. The man in the top hat has giantism, which is caused by a tumor on the gland that controls growth. The other man is a dwarf; dwarfism is a hereditary condition. The woman in the picture is of average size.

How Bones Grow

As your bones get longer, you are getting taller. But how does this actually happen? The answer is in the *cartilage,* that rubbery tissue that made up most of your baby skeleton.

By the time you turn fourteen, most of your cartilage will have been replaced by bone. However, some cartilage remains. Inside some of your bones there are two thin pads of cartilage, called *growth plates*. These growth plates, as the name suggests, make it possible for you to keep growing. Here's how: The inner edge of

Cartilage ——————— Spongy bone

Growth plate

The cartilage in a growth plate creates new cartilage as the old cartilage gradually turns to spongy bone. The new cartilage extends the length of the bone. It will eventually turn to bone and be replaced by more new cartilage.

the growth plate *ossifies,* or becomes bone. Meanwhile, new cartilage grows along the outer edge of the growth plates. This new cartilage makes the bone longer. Growing stops when all the growth plates completely turn to bone.

Growth takes place everywhere within a child's bone, which is almost all cartilage.

growth plate — 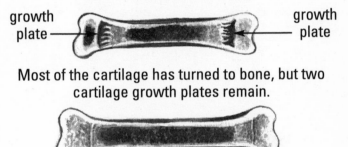 → growth plate

Most of the cartilage has turned to bone, but two cartilage growth plates remain.

There is minimal growth in adult bones.

Many different factors determine how tall you will grow to be, including how tall your parents are. Stretching yourself on the jungle gym won't make you taller. In fact, there is not much you can do to affect your height. But one factor that you can control is the food you eat. Eating protein, for example, is especially important while you are still growing because it is one of the basic building blocks for new *tissue*.

Tissue is a group of similar cells that form an organ or other body part. For example, muscle tissue is made up of muscle cells.

> With help from muscles, bones can move up, down, and all around.

Chapter 3
Bones on the Move

Jumping, skipping, chewing, throwing a ball, writing, hugging, waving — these movements, and thousands more, are part of your everyday life. You do them without even thinking about it. But have you ever stopped to wonder how your body moves? It seems easy, but moving actually requires that your brain, nerves, muscles, and bones all work together. Even just the simple task of picking up a pencil can be a complicated process.

If you want to pick up a pencil, you just reach out, grab it, and lift. No problem. But before your hand actually moves, a lot of steps happen very quickly:

•Your brain decides that you want to pick something up.
•Your brain quickly decides what response is needed.

Move hand.

•Your brain sends impulses or messages down nerve cells through the spinal cord to nerve endings in your muscles.

•Your muscles go into action, and your body moves in response.

How Muscles Move Bones

Just as you work with teammates to score a goal or shoot a basket, your bones and muscles work as a team to move your body. Each time you decide to move, your muscles contract and pull a bone, or bones, with them. To get a sense of how muscles work with bones, hold your arm out straight, then bend your elbow to bring your hand closer to your body. This is called *flexing*. When you straighten your arm again, you are *extending*. Feel the biceps muscle tighten

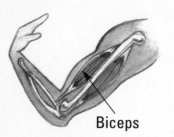

Biceps

when you flex your arm. Feel the triceps tighten when you extend. Tough, stretchy bands, called *tendons,* attach your muscles to your bones. They also attach muscles to other muscles. So when you flex your arm, the

Triceps

Your biceps and triceps work together to move your forearm.

attached tendons pull against your arm bones, making them move at the *elbow joint*. A joint is the place where two or more bones come together.

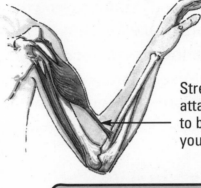

Stretchy tendons attach muscles to bones to help you move.

Muscle Motion

Although your muscles and bones work together to help you move in many different ways, each muscle can only do one thing: *contract*. Contract means to tighten and shorten. As a muscle tightens and shortens, it pulls the bone with it. But the muscle can't push the bone away again, so there is another set of muscles to move the bones the other way. Muscles work in pairs, one to pull a bone one way (extending), and the other to pull it back again (flexing).

Your body has more than 600 muscles that help your skeleton move.

Muscles need oxygen to move. The harder muscles are working, the more oxygen they need. Blood carries oxygen to the muscles.

Joints: A Meeting Place

The places where your bones come together are called joints. Bones are held together at the joints by *ligaments,* which are like strong pieces of string. Some joints, like most of the ones in the skull, hold your bones together so that they don't move. Other joints, like your elbow, allow your bones to move. Your body has several different kinds of joints that help you to move in various ways.

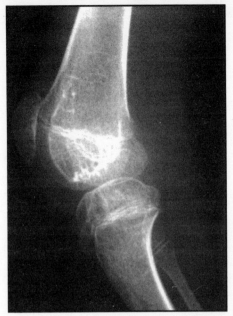

Joint effort: This is an elbow joint. Joints help your bones move in different ways.

Cartilage Is a Cushion

Soft pads of cartilage between moving joints help make movement smooth and painless. When the cartilage between the joints wears down, osteoarthritis can develop. (This arthritis is a painful condition that is caused by bones grinding against one another, because there is very little cartilage to cushion the joint.)

Hinge Joints

When you pump your legs to make a swing go higher, you are using your knee joint. Like an elbow, the knee is a hinge joint. You can find other hinge joints in your fingers and toes.

Elbow

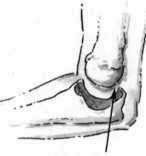

Hinge joint

The hinge joint got its name because it moves like a door hinge — it swings open to 180 degrees, and it can only swing back and forth.

Neat Knees

The knee is the biggest and strongest joint in the body. It connects the thighbone (femur) to the lower leg bones (tibia and fibula). The knee joint can also lock the leg in a straight line and hold the weight of the entire body.

That knee is one swinging joint!

Hinge joint

Ball-and-Socket Joints

A *ball-and-socket joint* is named for the way it looks — a rounded, ball-like

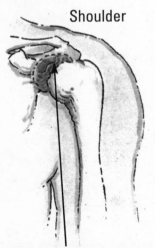

Shoulder

Ball-and-socket joint

part at the end of a bone fits into a cuplike socket of the connecting bone. This type of joint is found in your hip and shoulder. Ball-and-socket joints allow you to move not only back and forth, but also around in a circle. Try it!

A socket is a hole or hollow place where something fits in. In a ball-and-socket joint, the rounded end of the bone fits right into the joint's socket.

Sliding Joints

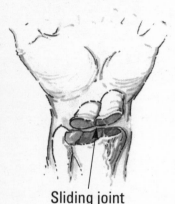

Your wrists and ankles are called *sliding joints,* because the bones slide over one another to move. The sliding joint gives wrists and ankles a lot of ways to move.

Sliding joint

Saddle Joints

The *saddle joint* that connects your thumb to your hand looks like a horse's saddle, which is how it got its name. This useful joint allows you to move your thumb from side to side and back to front.

Saddle joint

26

Pivot Joints

Your neck bones meet at *pivot joints,* which let you rotate your head and turn it from side to side.

Pivot joint

There are other joints that have more complicated jobs, but these are the most common.

No More Squeaky Joints

Inside your joints, a substance called synovial fluid keeps your bones from rubbing together. Just like oil keeps your bike from getting squeaky, synovial fluid "oils" your joints so they move smoothly.

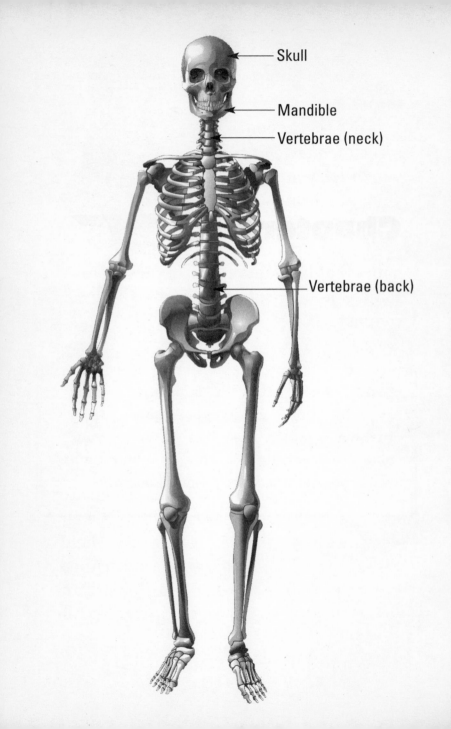

Hey, bonehead! That's right, you're a bonehead. I'm one, too. And that's a good thing.

Chapter 4

Skull, Spine, and Neck

Skull

Your head is literally made up of bones — twenty-nine of them in all. Together, they're called a skull. Your head bones sit on top of your neck bone (which is part of your backbone). The reason your skull feels like one large bone instead of twenty-nine separate ones is because the bones fit together very tightly. These bones are held together by nonmoving joints called sutures. Your skull has the important job of protecting your brain and your sense organs, including your eyes, nose, ears, and tongue.

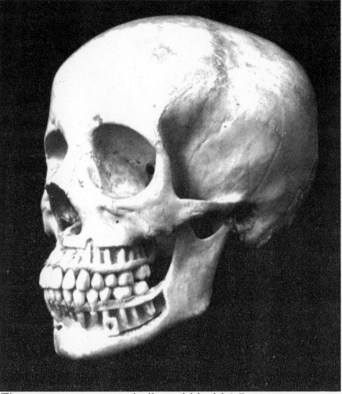

The average empty skull could hold 1.5 quarts.

Touch the top of your head, and you'll feel a hard bowl shape called the *cranium.* Your cranium covers your brain the way a construction worker's hard hat covers her head. The cranium alone is made up of eight separate bones.

It doesn't hurt to be hardheaded!

Soft Heads

The cranium of a newborn baby has gaps called *soft spots* or *fontanels*, which allow the baby's head to be squeezed slightly as it passes through the narrow birth canal. As the baby grows, these gaps close tightly.

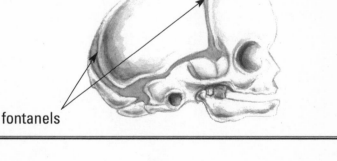

fontanels

A baby's head seems big because it _is_ big! A baby's skull makes up one-fourth of its body. But by the time the baby becomes a grown-up, the skull is only one-eighth of the full body.

Fourteen bones shape your face. If you gently feel around your eyes, you can feel your eye sockets — the holes in your skull where your eyes fit. More than half of the eyeball is actually hidden behind your skull, which protects it.

Your nose is protected by the flexible cartilage that is located at its end. This cartilage is like a cushion — it can flatten out if you bump into something. Even though most of your nose is cartilage, it can still break — especially at the top where it is bone.

Your lower jawbone, or _mandible,_ is the only bone in your head that moves. Without it, you would have a hard time talking and eating. The mandible is also the largest and strongest bone in your face. Your two upper jawbones, called the *maxillae,* or *maxillary bones,* form most of your face and the roof of your mouth, but unlike the mandible, they can't move.

The Truth About Teeth

Teeth are attached to your skull, but they are not bones. They are strong, though. Enamel, the 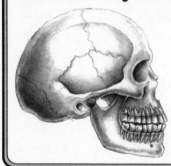 outer layer of teeth, is the hardest substance in the body — even harder than bones. Because teeth are rooted to bone, they stay attached — even after the body decomposes.

Spine

What is a vertebrate? Cats, dogs, fish, birds, pigs, monkeys, bears, mice, people, and thousands of other animals are all vertebrates. That means they have a backbone, or spine. Without your spine, you wouldn't be able to stand up straight. It's your body's main support.

Kids have thirty-three separate back bones, or *vertebrae,* which fit together at separate joints. But grown-ups have only

7 neck
vertebrae

Upper
back

Lower
back—
5 vertebrae

Sacrum—
5 vertebrae
often fused
together

Coccyx—
3–5
vertebrae
often fused
together

Your spine protects your spinal cord.

twenty-six—some of them fuse together as you grow. The joints in your spine allow you to twist, turn, and bend. The vertebrae fit one on top of the other all the way up your back. There is a hole through each bone. This hole creates the spinal canal, which protects the spinal cord. Working with the brain, the spinal cord sends messages throughout the body telling muscles to move.

Between each vertebra and the next is a jellylike disk of cartilage that cushions your spine.

34

Many medical words, including the names of bones, come from Latin. Latin was the language of the ancient Romans. The Roman empire was very powerful and Latin became the universal language

People still use Latin for medical terms. The word *vertebra* (plural: *vertebrae*) comes from the Latin word *vertere*, which means "to turn." That makes sense—your many vertebrae allow your body to turn and twist.

From the side, your spine looks like a long "S" shape, with curves bending toward the back of your body and toward the front. The curves help strengthen your backbone, balance your body, and absorb shocks.

The last three to five vertebrae form the coccyx, which is commonly known as the tailbone. This is actually the remains of a tail, which disappeared with evolution.

Every night you are just a fraction of an inch shorter than you were when you woke up. Just as a cushion gets squashed when you sit on it, so do the cartilage pads in your spine during a day's activities. While you sleep, the pads become cushiony and plump again.

Neck

Your neck bones are really just an extension of your backbone. The seven vertebrae in your neck rotate so you can turn your head from side to side. Muscles in the back of your neck connect the bottom of your skull to the upper neck vertebrae.

Humans and giraffes have the same number of bones in their necks. The giraffe's bones are just much longer.

Your shoulder bone is connected to your arm bone. Well, it's just a little more complicated than that.

Chapter 5

Shoulders and Arms

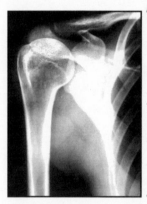

The primary purpose of your shoulders is to connect your arms to your body. Each of your shoulders is made up of three separate bones: the *scapula* (plural: *scapulae)*, the *clavicle*, and the *humerus*.

The scapulae, or shoulder blades, are two large, flat, triangular bones. Each shoulder blade is connected to the top of your rib cage by one of your clavicles, or collarbones. The other end of each collarbone is connected to the breastbone, or *sternum*. Together your collarbones and shoulder blades form the support system from which your upper arm bones hang.

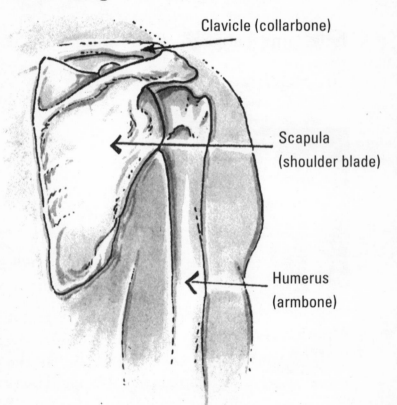

Clavicle (collarbone)

Scapula
(shoulder blade)

Humerus
(armbone)

Back of the shoulder

The very end of your shoulder is actually the top of your upper arm bone, called the *humerus*.

Arms

The humerus, the thick bone that goes from your shoulder to your elbow, is long and strong. The humerus is attached to the shoulder by a ball-and-socket joint, which allows the upper arm to move up, down, and all around. The strong muscles of the upper arm and shoulder also help hold the humerus in place.

The Funniest Bone

The "funny bone" isn't a bone — and it isn't that funny, either. It's actually a nerve at the back of your elbow. If you've ever banged it, you know that it can really hurt! As you might have guessed, it's called "funny" because the nerve has the same name, *humerus*, as the bone in your upper arm, and *humerus* sounds like *humorous*.

The humerus is connected to two lower arm bones called the *ulna* and the *radius*. You can feel the radius on the thumb side of your arm. The ulna is on the other side. The way these two bones work together gives your lower arm greater flexibility and allows it to twist at the wrist.

When your palm is facing up, the ulna and radius are in a straight line. When the arm is moved so that the palm is facing down, the two lower arm bones form an "X" shape.

The three arm bones meet at the elbow, which is a hinge joint. Without your elbow, you couldn't throw a ball, do push-ups, answer the phone, or do a whole lot of other things. The muscles below your elbow control movement of your lower arm and wrist, while muscles above your elbow let you raise and lower your arm.

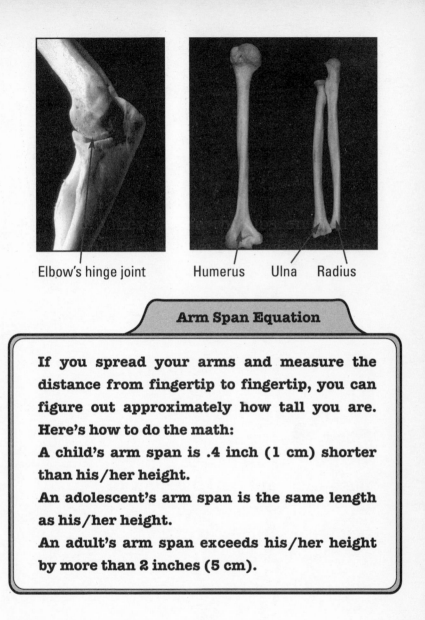

Elbow's hinge joint   Humerus   Ulna   Radius

Arm Span Equation

If you spread your arms and measure the distance from fingertip to fingertip, you can figure out approximately how tall you are. Here's how to do the math:

A child's arm span is .4 inch (1 cm) shorter than his/her height.

An adolescent's arm span is the same length as his/her height.

An adult's arm span exceeds his/her height by more than 2 inches (5 cm).

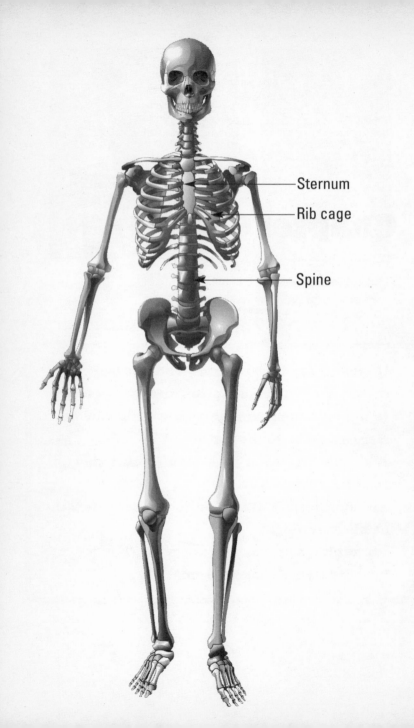

Sternum

Rib cage

Spine

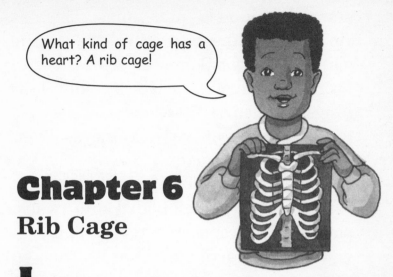

What kind of cage has a heart? A rib cage!

Chapter 6
Rib Cage

Just as your spine protects your spinal cord and your skull protects your brain, your ribs protect some very important body parts, too: your heart, spleen, liver,

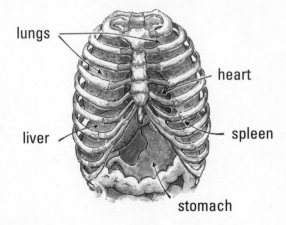

lungs

heart

liver

spleen

stomach

stomach, kidneys, and lungs. The flat rib bones connect to other bones—the spine and breastbone, or *sternum* — to form a protective cage around your lungs and heart. These curved bones also protect parts of your kidneys, liver, spleen, and stomach.

Altogether you have twenty-four separate rib bones, divided into twelve pairs. All are connected to the spine in your back. Cartilage connects the top seven pairs of ribs directly to the sternum. The next three pairs, called "false ribs," are shorter than the others. They are attached to the sternum and the ribs

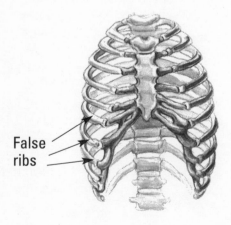

The rib cage from the front

False ribs

above them by a cartilage band. The bottom two pairs of ribs are called "floating ribs" because they only attach to the backbone, so from the front they appear to be floating.

As you breathe, your ribs move to allow your lungs to fill with air. Feel your ribs as you breathe in deeply and breathe out again. Your rib cage is strong but flexible. The ribs are lifted upward and move slightly apart as your lungs expand. Also, the breastbone (sternum) moves forward, too. When you exhale, the muscles around your ribs relax, so the ribs return to their original position.

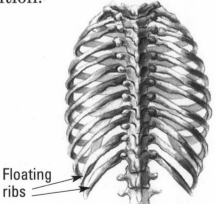

The rib cage from the back

All of the ribs are attached to the spine.

Floating ribs

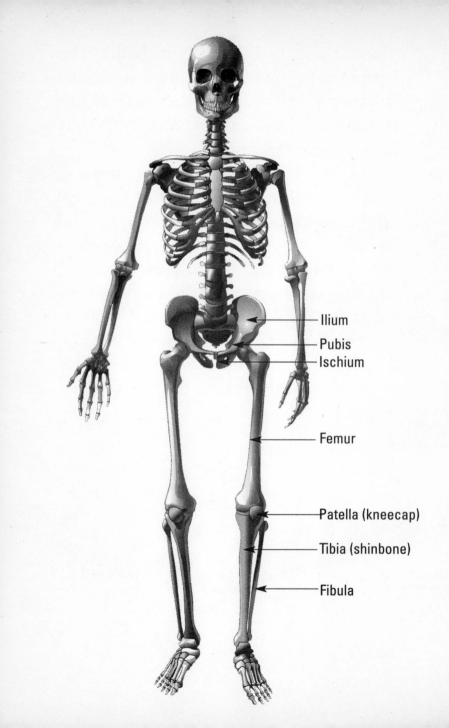

Ilium

Pubis

Ischium

Femur

Patella (kneecap)

Tibia (shinbone)

Fibula

> Hip, hip, hooray! Your hips and legs help you stand upright and move around.

Chapter 7
Hips and Legs

Your hipbones form your pelvis, which is shaped like a basin. (A basin is a wide, shallow bowl.) This curved shape keeps your legs in line with the top half of your body to support much of your weight and to help you keep your balance. Without hips, you wouldn't be able to stand upright or move around. Your pelvis also protects the organs inside your lower body.

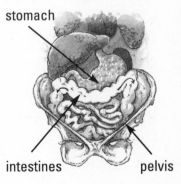

stomach

intestines

pelvis

Pelvis is the Latin word for "basin."

The pelvis is made up of two sets of three bones. The part that you can feel on each side, just below your waist, is the *ilium*. The *ischium* is in your buttocks. And the *pubis* bone is in the lower front part of your body. At birth, these three hipbones are separate, but by the time you are a teenager, they'll have fused together into one bone. The two hipbones meet on either side of the lower part of your spine.

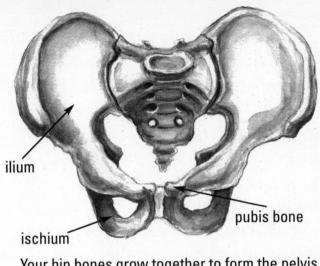

ilium

ischium

pubis bone

Your hip bones grow together to form the pelvis.

Not All Pelvises Are the Same

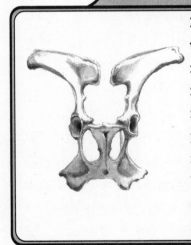

Because humans walk upright, their pelvis is rounder than that of animals that walk on all four legs. This is a cow's pelvis. Its back legs fit into the round sockets. You can see the difference between this and a human pelvis.

Legs

A ball-and-socket joint connects your legs to your pelvis. Looking at a skeleton, it is easy to see the rounded end at the top of the thighbone, or *femur.* The rounded end fits perfectly into the cuplike socket created by the hipbones. The femur is the longest and heaviest bone in your whole body.

Like your lower arm, your lower leg is made up of two smaller bones, the *tibia* and the *fibula.* The tibia is the wider of these two bones. It may be small, but it is one of the body's strongest bones. The tibia is also known as the shinbone or shin. The fibula is the thinner of the two lower leg bones. It helps control ankle movement.

It's important to protect your tibia when you play soccer.

Try swinging your leg back and forth, and you'll know right away that your knee is a hinge joint connecting the femur to your lower leg

50

bones. This joint is what allows you to kick, jump, squat, dance, and much more. Protecting this important joint is your kneecap, or *patella*.

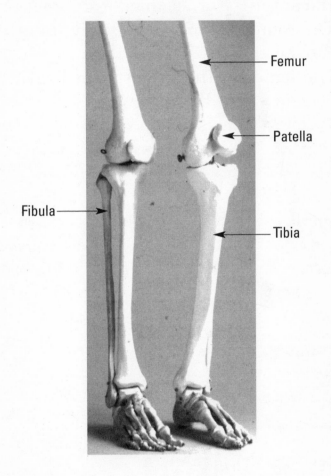

Femur

Patella

Fibula

Tibia

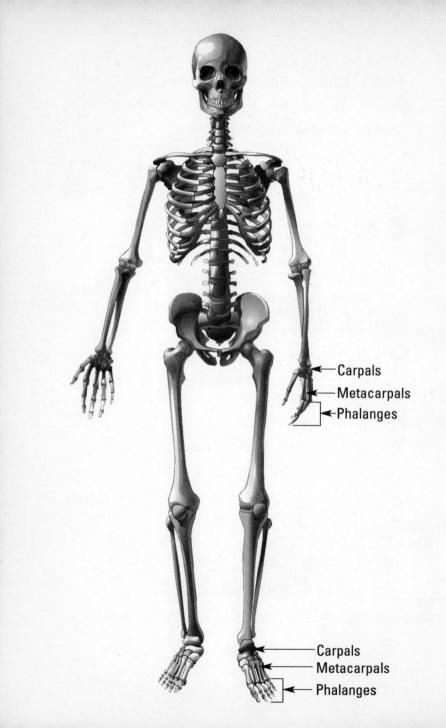

Carpals
Metacarpals
Phalanges

Carpals
Metacarpals
Phalanges

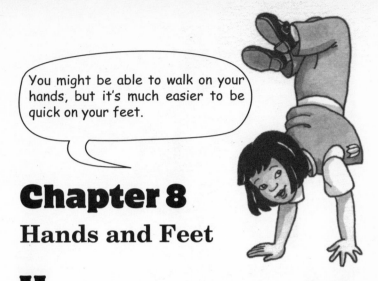

You might be able to walk on your hands, but it's much easier to be quick on your feet.

Chapter 8
Hands and Feet

Hands and feet are very good at doing their jobs. If you wiggle your hands and feet, you will notice how flexible they are and how many ways you can move them. That's because they are made up of lots of bones and joints. With twenty-six bones in each foot and twenty-seven in each hand, more than half the bones in your body are in your hands and feet.

Hands
The twenty-seven bones in your hand are divided into three groups. One

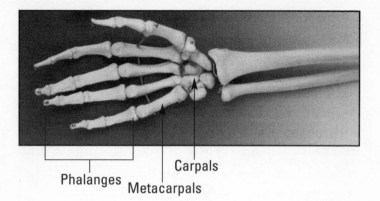

Phalanges Carpals Metacarpals

group includes the eight small wrist bones, called *carpals*. Carpal bones are arranged in two rows and are held together tightly by ligaments. The way the carpals fit together helps your wrist to be flexible and move in many directions. Connected to the carpals is a second group of bones, called *meta-carpals*. These five long bones make up the palm and back side of your hand. Finally, connected to your metacarpals are your finger bones, or *phalanges*. There are fourteen phalanges in each hand.

In the wrist, there is a narrow passageway of bones and ligaments called the *carpal tunnel.* Nerves, tendons, and blood vessels pass through this tunnel on their way to the fingers. People who use the computer all day (or do other jobs that require their fingers to make the same types of motions again and again) are at risk of irritating the carpal tunnel, which results in tingling, numbness, and pain in their hands.

When you sit at the computer for a long time, make sure your keyboard is at a comfortable height for you. You should also take frequent breaks to stretch and shake out your arms and hands.

Hands are good at grasping because of the way they're constructed. Each of your fingers is made up of three phalanges connected by hinge joints. With three joints in each finger, you can bend your fingers tightly toward the palm of your hand. Your thumb sits at an angle to your fingers. It has just two phalanges, but it is attached to your hand with a saddle joint. The saddle joint lets your thumb move back and forth and all around. Since your thumb can bend to touch the tips of your fingers, it makes it easy to grip even tiny objects.

Opposable Thumb

Scientists call the human thumb an "opposable thumb" because we can squeeze it against each of our other fingers. Having an opposable thumb helps us to do small, complicated movements, like threading a needle, writing, and picking up small objects.

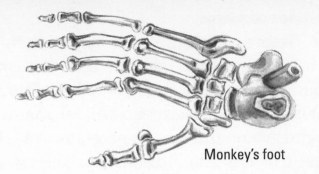

Monkey's foot

Monkeys have thumbs on their hands and feet — they can eat bananas with their toes!

Give that monkey a hand!

Ankles and Feet

Your foot bones support the weight of your entire body. Like the bones in your hands, your foot bones are divided into three groups. The seven ankle bones are called *tarsals,* and they make up the back of the foot. Sliding joints connect the tarsals in the ankle, allowing you to flex your feet so you can walk, climb, run, and dance.

> Your feet can bend as you walk, so you can walk on all kinds of surfaces.

The five *metatarsal* bones make up the middle part of your foot and connect the tarsals to your toe bones, which, like the finger bones, are also called *phalanges.* There are fourteen phalanges in each foot — the same number as in each hand. Finger bones and toe bones may share the same name, but they look and act quite differently. Unlike your slender finger bones, the phalanges in your toes are short and thick, which helps you balance on two feet. And, unlike your thumb, your big toe is set in a line with your other toes, and is connected by a hinge joint rather than a saddle joint, so it can't move against the rest of your toes. That's why you probably aren't as good at eating, sewing, or playing the piano with your toes.

Foot bones are flatter and longer than hand bones. Foot bones are arranged so the foot is flat and wide enough to help us stand upright and keep our balance.

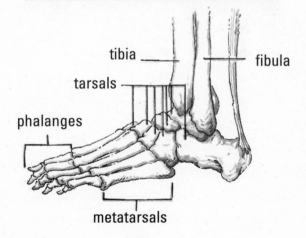

tibia

fibula

tarsals

phalanges

metatarsals

All About Arches

Everyone is born with flat feet, but as we walk, our muscles and ligaments become stronger and our foot bones rise to form an arch. The arch is important because it helps support the body's weight.

Sticks and stones may break my bones, but my bones can heal themselves!

Chapter 9

Broken Bones

We think of our bones as being strong and hard. But, as you probably know, they can break. Bones don't break easily — it takes a serious fall or accident to break one — but when they do break, it can really hurt! Some broken bones, or *fractures,* are more serious than others. In a *simple fracture,* for example, the bone breaks cleanly in two, but doesn't stick out of the skin. In more serious breaks, called *compound fractures,* the broken pieces of bone pierce through the skin.

This X ray shows a multiple fracture where both the tibia and fibula have been broken. Since your leg must carry a lot of weight, it can take up to six months to heal.

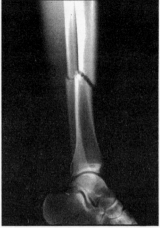

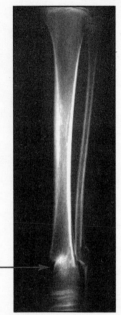

The hands, wrists, and forearm bones are the ones kids under twelve years old break most often. *Green-stick fractures,* when bones splinter on one side of the bone without breaking in two, are also common.

Here you can see a greenstick fracture, where one side of the bone is broken, and the other is just bent. The term "greenstick" comes from the way a young green tree branch tears on one side but stays attached on the other.

It's not easy to break bones. A 2-inch (5-cm) block of bone can hold the weight of an elephant.

Bone Repair

Broken bones may hurt a lot, but the good news is that with a little help from the doctor, bones have the amazing ability to heal themselves in as little as three weeks (though many breaks take longer to heal).

A broken bone repairs itself in three stages:

1. The first stage of healing involves a blood clot. Bones have blood vessels inside them, and when the bone breaks, the blood vessels do, too. When this happens, the bone bleeds. Very soon, the blood that comes out hardens and forms a clot around the broken ends, very much like the scab that forms when your skin is cut.

hardened blood

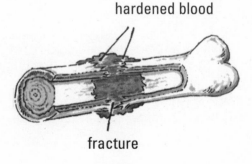

fracture

2. Next, minerals and bone-repairing tissues go to work building new, soft bone where the blood clot has formed. This new bone, called *callus,* is soft at first because it is made up of tissue and cartilage.

callus

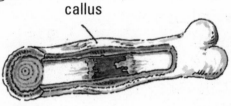

3. Finally, the callus grows between the broken ends of the bone and hardens. When it is completely hard, the bone is healed.

hardened callus

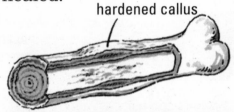

The word callus can also refer to a hard, thickened area of skin. Many people get calluses on their toes from walking and standing a lot.

To help the healing process, the doctor will sometimes put a plaster cast on the area where the broken bone is, to help hold it still and keep the pieces in place. More serious breaks may also require screws or pins to hold the bones together while they heal.

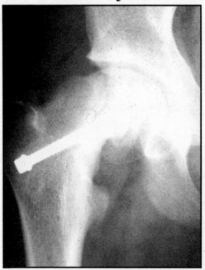

This picture shows a pin holding the femur in place. The injury will heal more quickly if the bone cannot move.

Sprains can hurt as much as broken bones, but they are not injuries to the bone. A sprain happens when a ligament is torn or stretched.

X-ray Vision

By sending X rays through your skin, doctors can see if a bone is broken. The X rays can't pass through bone, so bones appear white in X-ray pictures, or radiographs, while skin, fat, muscle, and everything else is dark. When the doctor examines the radiograph, she can see how bad the break is.

An X ray is really a picture of a bone's shadow.

Here's what you need to know about taking good care of your bones, from the inside out.

Chapter 10
Healthy Bones

Because your skeleton holds up your body and protects your organs, it is a very important part of leading a healthy life. If you make sure to take care of your bones, starting from the time you're young, it will help you prevent some health problems later in life.

Caring for your bones is easier than you might think. You are probably already doing it without even knowing it. Do you drink milk? Do you eat cheese and broccoli? Do you play sports? If you answered yes to most or all of these questions, you are already on the road to taking good care of your bones!

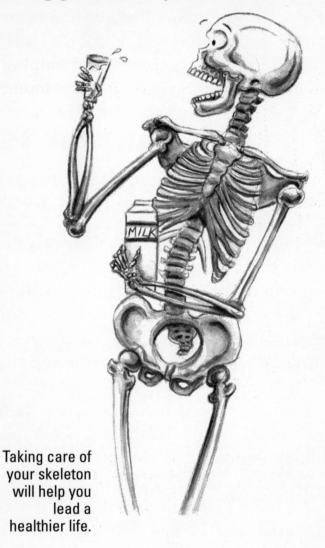

Taking care of your skeleton will help you lead a healthier life.

Exercising

Besides keeping your heart and lungs healthy, and making your muscles strong, exercise is also good for your bones. It can even play a role in helping you grow taller. Scientists have found that the more you exercise, the more your bones will grow, and the stronger they'll be.

People who are so sick that they have to spend a long time in bed can lose bone strength. Their bones grow thinner, weaker, and sometimes even smaller from being in bed all day. When they do get out of bed again, they are at a high risk of breaking their weak bones.

Muscles and joints keep your bones moving, so it's important that you take care of them, too. Starting each day with stretching exercises is a great way to keep your muscles and joints from getting stiff. Even a little exercise is better than none in keeping muscles and bones healthy.

Eating Healthy

Cookies, candy, soda, chips — these may be some of your favorite treats, but for your bones' sake, it's important to limit the junk, and maintain a healthy diet. Minerals such as calcium and phosphorus are key to healthy bones. This chart lists some important vitamins and minerals and some foods that contain them.

The Benefits of Vitamins and Minerals

Vitamin/Mineral

Phosphorus

Food Source

Yogurt, corn, ice cream, milk, nuts, oatmeal, sardines, bran, asparagus, spinach, beans, cheese, sweet potatoes

Benefits

Builds strong teeth and bones

Vitamin/Mineral

Calcium

Food Source

Milk, yogurt, cheese, vegetables, meat, poultry, fish, dried beans, eggs, nuts, fruits, bread, cereal, rice, pasta

Benefits

Keeps bones strong
Helps blood to clot, muscles to contract, and nerves to carry messages to muscles

Vitamin/Mineral

Vitamin A

Food Source

Whole eggs, whole milk, liver, tomatoes, carrots, cantaloupes, apricots

Benefits

Helps vision, bone growth, cell division
Enhances the body's ability to fight disease

Vitamin/Mineral

Vitamin C

Food Source

Citrus fruits, strawberries, kiwi, black currants, papaya, red peppers, broccoli, brussels sprouts, tomatoes, cantaloupes, cauliflower, leafy green vegetables

Benefits

Supports and protects blood vessels, joints, bones, teeth, tendons, organs, corneas, ligaments, cartilage
Helps with healing of wounds, fractures, and bruises

Vitamin/Mineral

Vitamin D

Food Source

Fortified milk, meat, eggs, oily fish (sardines, salmon, tuna)

Benefits

Helps the body absorb calcium
Helps produce white blood cells

Rickets

Not getting enough vitamin D can cause rickets — a condition in which growing bones become soft because they didn't get enough minerals. Sunlight helps your body make vitamin D, so go outside!

Your skeleton is an important and living part of your body that lets you breathe, eat, talk, move, dance, run, and play. You could not live without it, so be sure to take care of your bones through exercise and healthy eating.

VERTEBRATES

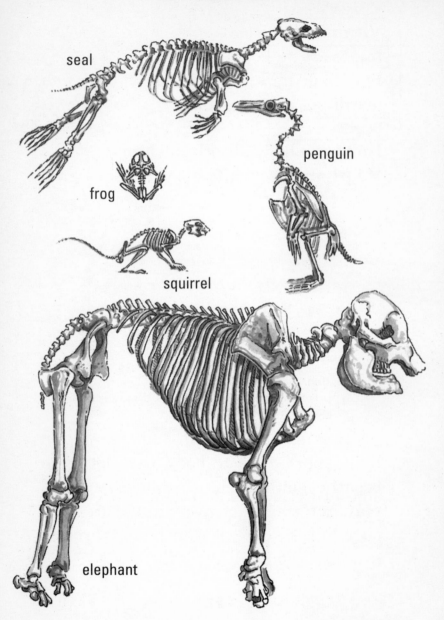

seal

frog

penguin

squirrel

elephant

Skeletons come in all shapes and sizes, just like animals.

Chapter 11
Animal Bones

Each animal's skeleton matches its specific lifestyle. Humans have rounded hips that help them stand up straight. Elephants have thick leg bones to support their enormous bodies. Squirrels have front paws for grasping nuts and a long tail for balancing in the trees, while seals have broad flippers that help them swim. Some animals don't even have skeletons, and that works well for them, too.

Vertebrates

Humans are vertebrates, which

means that they all have a backbone. You can find vertebrates throughout the animal kingdom. Fish, amphibians, and reptiles are vertebrates, as well as birds and mammals. Having a backbone enables these animals to stand up and move around. Their spine supports the rest of their skeleton.

Some vertebrates, like your pet dog or cat, have the same type of skeleton as you. You may not look much like your dog or cat, but you both have a skull, four limbs, and a spine.

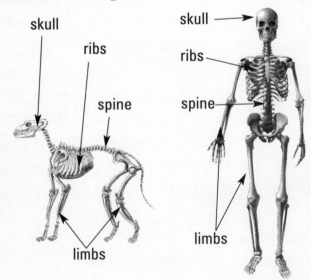

skull

ribs

spine

limbs

skull

ribs

spine

limbs

Other vertebrates have skeletons that are very different from human skeletons.

Fish have some of the same parts that we do, such as a skull and a spinal column. But in most fish, the rest of their bones extend straight out from the spine in two flat rows, kind of like a two-sided comb. And instead of arms and legs, they have fins, which are better for swimming. Most fins are made of cartilage rather than bone. In fact, many fish have skeletons made entirely of cartilage.

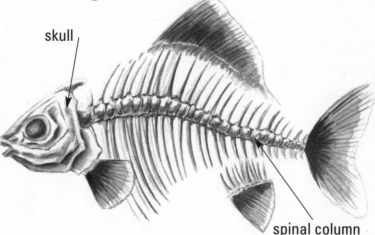

skull

spinal column

Bird bones are also quite different from ours. They are much lighter in weight. Some are actually hollow — which helps birds to fly.

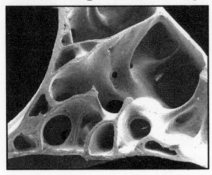

This is the skull bone of a falcon. The hollow design is just as strong as solid bone but much lighter.

A boa constrictor skeleton has a skull, but it doesn't have much else in common with a human skeleton—except a very long backbone. The boa has many bones in its back to help it slither around and curl up.

Fish are the oldest vertebrates. They first appeared about 500 million years ago. Fish were the only vertebrates until around 360 million years ago when amphibians developed.

Fun with Fossils

We know a lot about prehistoric vertebrates because of their fossils. Bones and teeth are strong and durable. They can last millions of years, while the soft parts of our body decay fairly quickly. Over time, mud and sand cover the hard parts of an animal's body. The minerals in the mud and sand soak into the bones and teeth, making them as hard as a rock. Eventually, the bones and teeth become fossils.

INVERTEBRATES

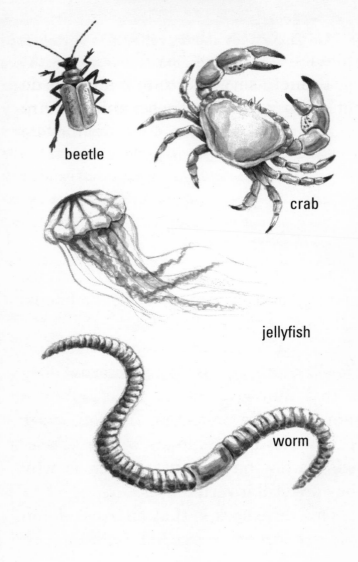

beetle

crab

jellyfish

worm

Invertebrates

Though there are many vertebrates roaming Earth, there are even more animals that do not have backbones. At least ninety-seven percent of animals do not have a spine. These animals are called invertebrates, and they include worms, jellyfish, and insects.

Some invertebrates, like worms and jellyfish, don't need a hard skeleton to move. They simply change their shape to get where they need to go.

Many other invertebrates, like crabs, lobsters, and insects, do have skeletons, but they're on the outside of the body. Outside skeletons are called *exoskeletons*. Exoskeletons are similar to internal ones in that they give the body strength and support, while protecting the soft, inner organs. However, animals with exoskeletons do not have spines, which is why they are still invertebrates.

One drawback is that an exoskeleton does not stretch or expand. Animals with exoskeletons have to shed their old skeletons and make new, larger ones to fit their growing bodies. When they first shed, their new skeleton is still soft and needs time to thicken and become hard.

Animals with exoskeletons are among the oldest in the world. The ancestors of cockroaches lived millions of years before dinosaurs. A cockroach's exoskeleton is made of chitin — a material a lot like your fingernails.

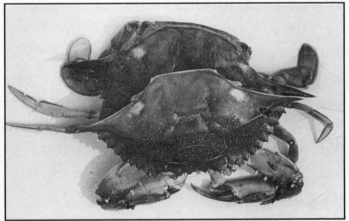

This crab is shedding its old skeleton. This process is called *molting.*

A Skeletal Summary

As you can see, animal skeletons come in all shapes and sizes. And, some have no skeleton at all! Other animals have exoskeletons, which are on the outside of their bodies. Inside or outside, all skeletons have one thing in common: They give the body a framework and help protect it.

INDEX

size of, 3

Fibula, 24, 50, 51, 59

Fingers, 24

        in grasping, 56–57

Fish, 77–79

Flexing, 20, 21

Fontanels, 31

Foods, for healthy bones, 67–73

Foot

        arches of, 60

        bones of, 58–59

        function of, 53

Forearm, muscles in movement of, 20-21

Fossils, 78–79

Fractures, 61–66

Funny bone, 39

Giantism, 13

Giraffe, neck bones of, 36

Growth, 10, 11–16

        factors in, 15–16

        in early years of life, 11–12

Growth disorders, 13

Growth hormones, 12–13

Growth plates, 14–15

Hands

        bones in, 53–54

        function of, 53

        in grasping, 56–57

Head, bones of, 29–33

Healing process, 63–65

Health, 67

        exercise for, 69–70

        foods for, 67–73, 70–73

Height, factors affecting, 15–16

Hinge joints, 24, 40, 50–51

of foot, 59
of hands, 56
Hipbones, 47–49
Humerus, 37, 38-39, 41

Ilium, 48, 49
Invertebrates, 2, 80, 81–83
Ischium, 48, 49

Jawbones, 32–33
Jellyfish, 80
Joints
      of arm, 38–39
      cartilage cushions in, 23
      elbow, 20–21, 23, 40, 41
      finger, 56–57
      of foot, 58–59
      health of, 69–70
      hip, 50
      knee, 50–51
      in movement, 22–27
      nonmoving, 29
      of spine, 33–34
      synovial fluid in, 26
      types of, 24–27
      wrist, 40

Knee joint, 24, 50–51

Legs, bones of, 50–51
Ligaments, 22
      spraining of, 65

Mandible, 32
Marrow, bone, 4–6, 8–10
      producing blood cells, 8–9
Maxillae (maxillary bones), 32–33

Pubis bones, 48, 49

Radius, 40, 41
Red blood cells, 9
Rib cage, 43–45
    protecting organs, 7–8
Rickets, 73

Sacrum, 48–49
Saddle joints, 26, 56
Scapula, 37
Seals, 74, 75
Shoulders, 25, 37–38
Skeleton. See also Bones
    of birds, 78
    of fish, 77
    function of, 1
    number of bones in, 2–4
    variety of, 76–77, 83
Skull, 29–33
    of baby, 31–32
    of falcon, 78
    protecting brain, 7
Sliding joints, 26, 58
Spinal cord, 19, 33–34
Spine, 33–35. See also Vertebrae
    cartilage in, 34, 36
    protecting nerves, 7
    ribs connected to, 44
    in vertebrates, 76–78
Spongy bone, 4, 5, 6
Sprains, 65
Squirrels, 74, 75
Sternum, 38, 44
Stirrup, size of, 3–4
Sutures, 29
Synovial fluid, 26

Photo credits:

p. 5 Biophoto Associates/Photo Researchers, Inc.; p. 13 Science Photo Library/Photo Researchers, Inc.; p. 14 Biophoto Associates/Photo Researchers, Inc.; p. 23 Martin M. Rotker/Photo Researchers, Inc.; p. 30 John Watney/Photo Researchers, Inc.; p. 37 Biophoto Associates/Photo Researchers, Inc.; p. 41 (left), James Stevenson/Science Photo Library/ Photo Researchers, Inc.; p. 41 (right) Video Surgery/Photo Researchers, Inc.; p. 51 David Young-Wolff/Photo Edit; Astrid and Hanns-Frieder Michler/Science Photo Library/Photo Researchers, Inc.; p. 62 (left) Biophoto Associates/Photo Researchers, Inc.; p. 62 (right) Department of Clinical Radiology, Salisbury District Hospital/Science Photo Library/Photo Researchers, Inc.; p. 65 Dr. P. Marazzi/Science Photo Library/Photo Researchers, Inc.; p. 78 Oliver Meckes/Photo Researchers, Inc.; p. 79 Superstock; p. 82 (top) Lynwood M. Chace/Photo Researchers, Inc.; p. 82 (bottom) Richard Frear/Photo Researchers, Inc.